For my parents,

who are always there for me whenever I need

them and who have taught me some of the

most valuable lessons I know.

FOREWORD

Electronic devices are a necessary part of modern life, but learning to use them wisely can be a challenge for both children and adults. *Tanya's Tech Troubles* offers an engaging and compassionate story of one child's journey toward electronic overuse and the resulting consequences for her personal and social well-being. With remarkable insight, author and high school student Danya Belkin recognizes that both parents and children contribute to the slippery slope of electronic overuse, and both are responsible for the solution. I recommend that families read this book before purchasing electronic devices. But for those who are already down the rabbit hole, *Tanya's Tech Troubles* offers an excellent tool for starting a conversation about electronic overuse, and taking steps to help children and adults restore balance to their lives. With Belkin's concise prose and Corbin Hillam's charming illustrations, this book will be a valuable addition to any home or classroom library, especially for children ages 5 to 12. In today's digital world where overuse of electronic devices can interfere with emotional growth and social relationships, *Tanya's Tech Troubles* can help families recognize signs of overuse, and take steps to foster healthier technology habits at home and at school.

– Nancy Collins, Ph.D., Professor, Psychological and
Brain Sciences, University of California, Santa Barbara

www.mascotbooks.com

Tanya's Tech Troubles

©2017 Danya Belkin. All Rights Reserved. No part of this publication may be reproduced, stored in a retrieval system or transmitted in any form by any means electronic, mechanical, or photocopying, recording or otherwise without the permission of the author.

For more information, please contact:
Mascot Books
560 Herndon Parkway #120
Herndon, VA 20170
info@mascotbooks.com

tanyastechtroubles@gmail.com

Library of Congress Control Number: 2017910199

CPSIA Code: PRT0917A
ISBN-13: 978-1-68401-528-3

Printed in the United States

TANYA'S TECH TROUBLES

written by **Danya Belkin**

illustrated by **Corbin Hillam**

Tanya Presswald loves her tablet. She can play her favorite games, watch the movies that she likes, and browse the Internet.

Day after day, she spends hours on her tablet. Every morning when she wakes up, the first thing she does is turn on her tablet to get a little time in before school. As she eats her breakfast, she uses her free hand to play on her tablet. She heads to school with her tablet in hand.

One time while texting at the grocery store, she bumped into a display of crackers, as her mom shouted, "Watch out!"

During another visit to the supermarket, Tanya's mom asked her to help carry the grocery bags to the car. Tanya was so focused on her tablet that she accidentally picked up another customer's grocery bag. The customer ran after Tanya, yelling at her to put down the bag!

Tanya's mom sees that the tablet helps calm Tanya and entertain her when she is bored or fidgety. Her mom likes the myriad of games and learning programs it offers. Her mom, after all, bought Tanya the tablet and encouraged Tanya to use it.

In some ways, the tablet is a babysitter. When Mrs. Presswald needs to do something important, like a business call, she says, "Tanya, where's your tablet? Please use it while I'm on the phone." That way, Tanya stays occupied and is not tempted to interrupt her mom during her work time.

Over dinner, the Presswald family used to talk about their days or discuss important family issues. These days, Tanya, and even her dad, focus on their electronic devices. They don't even lift their heads to make eye contact with the rest of the family. The dinner table is abnormally quiet.

After dinner one night, Tanya went to take her bath. She turned on the water to fill her bathtub. With her tablet in hand, she played a game while the tub filled. She became so intent on the game, she didn't notice the bathtub overflowing! Water was everywhere! Her rug was soaked, her shoes were drenched, and the floor looked like a river.

If Tanya is bored at home and doesn't feel like doing homework or chores, she pulls out the tablet and turns it on. Sometimes she doesn't realize hours have gone by until her mom or her dad calls.

"Tanya!" her father says. "You have been on the tablet all this time and you haven't taken out the trash, helped mom with dinner, or done any of your schoolwork!"

When Tanya goes to bed at night, she makes sure her tablet is charging on her nightstand. Often, as soon as her lights are out and her door is closed, she reaches for the bright screen, pulls it out of its charging area, and starts searching the Internet. The more time she spends browsing, the more trouble she has falling asleep. Her mind whirling, Tanya spends hours in her bed awake.

As the days and months pass, Tanya's family and friends notice that she has become irritable. Even the smallest annoyance really bothers her. But what upsets her most is when she is engrossed in her tablet and someone disturbs her.

At first, people thought Tanya's moodiness was simply part of growing up. As time passed, they realized that Tanya's bad moods were directly related to her overuse of electronics.

As the days go by, she even begins to ignore the people around her.

Riley, Tanya's best friend asks, "Hey! Tanya! Can you come over? I want you to meet my new puppy."

"Not now, Riley! I'm busy! Go away!"

"Tanya...Tanya? Hello!" Riley insists.

Tanya's head and body are frozen. Her fingers and eyes move as they slide up and down her tablet screen. She is in another world.

Riley feels sad. She does not ask Tanya to play with her anymore.

Riley's birthday is coming up. She is planning a party at the new ice skating rink for her closest friends. She decides not to invite Tanya.

"Riley," asks her mother, "are you sure you don't want to invite Tanya? She's been your best friend for such a long time!"

Riley nods. "I'm sure. Tanya has been ignoring me. If I don't invite her to my party, she will see how bad I feel."

Meanwhile, Tanya has been sneaking her tablet to school. One day, she wandered into a kindergarten class by mistake and sat down. Before she realized it, all the children were laughing at her.

Everyone, except Tanya, realizes that she is ADDICTED to her electronics.

Tanya feels stressed and anxious. When something bothers her, Tanya gets angry and can't calm herself down.

"Why doesn't anybody want to spend time with me? I don't have friends anymore. Family dinners are a blur. I can't even remember what I had for dinner last night."

Tanya's grades have fallen. Once a straight "A" student, Tanya got a "C" on her last math test.

Eventually, Mrs. McEamen, Tanya's teacher, catches Tanya using her tablet and confiscates it until the end of the day. Mrs. McEamen warns Tanya not to bring any electronics back to school. Tanya is embarrassed.

Tanya's parents are very concerned. Tanya used to be friendly and outgoing. Now she wants to be alone, avoids contact with her family and friends, and seems irritated by anyone who tries to interact with her. They notice her sleeplessness and anxiety.

After careful thought, Tanya's parents sit down and discuss their concerns with Tanya. They listen to Tanya as she expresses her feelings. "Mom and Dad, I know I have been using my tablet too often. My relationship with Riley is not as good as it used to be. My schoolwork is affected, and Mrs. McEamen has caught me using my tablet at school. I find it harder and harder to fall asleep at night, and I'm not as happy as I used to be. I need help. I want to feel good again."

Tanya's parents reassure Tanya that they are there to help and support her.

Together, they decide to set up a meeting with Mrs. McEamen to see if she can help.

During the meeting, Mrs. McEamen explains to Tanya and her parents, "Tanya is addicted to electronic devices. Addiction means Tanya cannot stop herself from using her tablet."

Mrs. McEamen adds, "Addiction to electronics is a growing problem. More and more, people find it hard to be social and make relationships with people outside the electronic world."

Tanya and her parents all want help. Tanya misses her friends, and her family misses her. Tanya agrees to spend shortened amounts of time on her tablet. Mrs. McEamen then sends the family home with a contract to control Tanya's overuse of electronics.

Her mother helps Tanya monitor her use of the tablet.

"Tanya, only 15 minutes please. Otherwise I will have to take the tablet away from you," her mom says. At first it is hard for Tanya to obey what her mother tells her.

Tanya's parents agree that no one will use electronic gadgets at the dinner table. Tanya and her family decide that on weekends they will play board games, solve puzzles together, visit local attractions, or see a movie. Tanya's mother will not use electronic gadgets to "babysit." Tanya will read a book when her mother needs to work.

Tanya asks Riley why she wasn't invited to Riley's birthday party.

"Tanya, you were always using your tablet! You haven't paid any attention to me! It really hurt my feelings when you ignored me."

Tanya apologized to her parents, Riley, and Mrs. McEamen. "I'm so sorry I ignored you. I promise to stop using my tablet so much."

Tanya will never again use her tablet so much. As Tanya and Riley have become best friends again, Tanya feels like her happy self again.

NOTE TO THE READER

Electronic devices are here to stay. We can't change that, but we can change how we treat these devices so that we use them far less.

Discussion Questions:

- Have you ever experienced a family member's overuse of an electronic device? If so, how did you feel about it?

- Have you ever tried talking to someone who wouldn't get off their phone? How did you feel?

- Why do you think Tanya wanted to stop using her tablet?

- Do you overuse an electronic device? If so, how do you think you can limit your use?

- What ideas do you have to help children minimize their use of electronics? How can parents or teachers help them?

- What do you think would be a fair contract to limit electronic use?

GLOSSARY OF IMPORTANT TERMS

Addiction – a strong and harmful need to have something or do something

Anxiety – fear or nervousness about what might happen

Depression – a state of feeling sad

Interpersonal Relationship – a strong, deep, or close association or acquaintance between two or more people

Irritability – a tendency to become angry or annoyed easily

Loneliness – sadness from being apart from other people

Stress – a state of mental tension and worry caused by problems in your life

ABOUT THE AUTHOR

Danya Belkin is a student at Dos Pueblos High School in Santa Barbara, California. She loves to help educate children and young adults about issues that affect them and their relationships.

AUTHOR'S COMMENTARY

Children and young adults use electronic devices to play games, browse the Internet, text, and interact on social media. The overuse of these electronic devices is ubiquitous. When I observed a change in the behavior of a number of my friends who were using these devices excessively, I conducted a study of the effects of overusing electronic gadgets. The results were frightening, and I felt they needed dissemination and discussion. I decided that a story for children, families, and their teachers would be appealing. My objective is to help children understand and conquer this serious problem of device addiction. In addition, I hope that the story will motivate families to discuss and change the way they use electronics.

ABOUT THE ILLUSTRATOR

Corbin Hillam has been a freelance illustrator for over 40 years. Most of his work is in the area of educational publishing for children. He has written and illustrated seven of his own books. He and his wife, Jane, live in Denver, Colorado to be close to their two granddaughters. He also enjoys hiking in Colorado's beautiful backcountry.

SPECIAL THANKS

Ryan Belkin, Leon Presser, Anita Presser, Linda Schwartz, Anne Gould, Deanna Robbins, Mary Hershey, Phyllis Amerikaner, Ann Lewin-Benham, Maria Chesley Fisk, Nancy Collins, Susan Epstein, Retired Teachers Association of Santa Barbara, City of Goleta, and The Safety Town Board